SCRUNCH THE UNIVERSE

by Seth Jarvis

Illustrated by Nathan Y. Jarvis

Published by Capstone Press, Inc.

Distributed By

 CHILDRENS PRESS®

CHICAGO

CIP
LIBRARY OF CONGRESS CATALOGING IN PUBLICATION DATA

Jarvis, Seth.
Scrunch the universe / by Seth Jarvis.
p. cm.--(Star Shows)
Summary: Uses models to depict the Sun, Earth, and other parts of
the solar system and galaxy.

ISBN 1-56065-010-9

1. Astronomy--Juvenile literature. 2. Sun--Models--Juvenile
literature. 3. Planets--Models--Juvenile literature. 4. Models and
modelmaking--Juvenile literature. [1. Astronomy. 2. Planets--
Models. 3. Solar system--Models. 4. Models and modelmaking.]
I. Title. II. Series.
QB46.J37 1989
523.2'0228--dc20   **89-25186 CIP AC**

Designed by Nathan Y. Jarvis & Associates, Inc.

Capstone Press

Box 669, Mankato, MN, U.S.A. 56001

CONTENTS

MODELS ARE USEFUL

THIS IS A BOOK about making models. It will teach you how to make models of outer space. You'll learn how to make models of the sun, Earth, moon, our solar system, and our galaxy. What you learn about how big they are and how far away they are may surprise you.

Everyone uses models of things. Kids play with model houses, cars, airplanes, you name it. They even play with models of people — dolls.

Adults use models, too. People who design buildings look at small models of what they are building. That helps them know how to construct it. Dentists make models of teeth that need fixing. Engineers make models of airplanes. Everyone makes or uses models. Models help you understand something. They let you look at the whole thing all at once. Models show you a picture.

Suppose you wanted to know how big Greenland is. Suppose you wanted to compare it with Great Britain. You could fly to Greenland, get out of the plane and look around. Then you could fly to Great Britain and do the same thing. You might have a nice vacation, but you really wouldn't get a feel for the sizes and shapes of these two islands.

You could look up Great Britain and Greenland in an encyclopedia. You could find out how many square miles or square kilometers they each have. The numbers might be interesting, but they're hard to picture. How big is Greenland? The encyclopedia says it is 2,192,500 square kilometers big. That's a huge number. But it doesn't give you a *feeling* for the size of Greenland. That big number doesn't tell you what shape Greenland is, either.

Now try this. Look at a globe of the Earth. A globe is a model. Find Greenland and Great Britain. On a globe, they are not too far from each other. Suddenly you can see their size and shape. All kinds of information is in front of you. *Useful* information. You can see that Greenland is a lot bigger than Great Britain. Greenland has a different shape than Great Britain. Greenland is much farther north than Great Britain. The longer you look at this model, the more you get a feeling for the differences in the sizes, shapes, and locations of these two islands. How long did it take? Not long at all. That's the great thing about models. They give lots of information. And they give it to you in a way that you can quickly understand.

This book will walk you through some easy arithmetic. It will be mostly multiplication and division. The arithmetic will help you figure out how to build your models. A simple pocket calculator will be handy. If you like to play with numbers, using a calculator will teach you a lot. If you don't have a calculator, that's fine. You don't need to do the math to learn from this book.

You'll see some very big numbers in this book. Here are some things you should remember:

1,000 times 1,000 equals
1,000,000 (a million)

1,000 times a million equals
1,000,000,000 (a billion)

1,000 times a billion equals
1,000,000,000,000 (a trillion)

Millions, billions, and trillions. All are used in making models of the universe.

Soon you can begin to make your models. But first there are three words you must understand. The words are *sphere*, *diameter*, and *circumference*. **Sphere** is pronounced like "fear" with an "s" tacked on at the front ("s-fear"). It means a perfectly round ball. **Diameter** is pronounced like "dye-AM-it-er." It means the width of a circle or sphere. **Circumference** is pronounced like "sir-COME-fur-ents." It is the distance around the outside of a circle or a sphere.

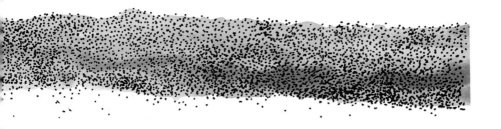

A MODEL OF THE EARTH AND THE MOON

See how this makes you feel: "The diameter of the Earth is 12,756 kilometers. The diameter of the moon is 3,476 kilometers. The distance between the two is 384,500 kilometers." Ugh. Lots of numbers. Those are useful numbers. But they don't really mean much by themselves. They don't give you a picture of the sizes of the Earth and moon and the distance between them.

This is where models come in handy. Your first project is to make a model of the Earth and the moon.

STEP ONE. First you have to decide what **scale** you want to use. The scale is the comparison between the model and the thing you make the model of. You must set the right scale. Ask yourself, "How big do I want the model to be when I'm finished?" If you set the scale too big, you are in for trouble. The Earth and moon will end up too big. Maybe as big as your house. Or your school! You can't build a model that big. You need a smaller scale.

You know that both the Earth and the moon are round. Why not set the scale of your model so that the Earth is as big as a basketball? Now *this* looks like it might be interesting. You've chosen a workable scale: The Earth shrunk to the size of a basketball.

STEP TWO. Now you need to figure out something called a **ratio**. You pronounce ratio like "RAY-she-oh." A ratio is a number that says how much bigger or smaller one thing is compared to another. Here's an example. You probably know that there are one hundred centimeters in a meter. This means that a meter is one hundred times longer than a centimeter. The ratio between meters and centimeters is written as 1:100. That means "one to a hundred."

Try another example. There are a thousand meters in a kilometer. This means that the ratio between kilometers and meters is 1:1,000. That means "one to a thousand."

One last example. A classroom has 20 students and one teacher. What is the ratio of students to teachers? "Twenty to one," or 20:1.

The order you use when you write down a ratio is very important. It has to be the same order you use when you describe the things you're comparing. The ratio of students to teachers is 20:1, but the ratio of teachers to students is 1:20. See the difference?

Now, what is the ratio between the size of the Earth and the size of the moon? The

Earth's diameter is 12,756 km. ("Km" stands for kilometers.) The moon's diameter is 3,476 km. The ratio between the Earth and moon would be 12,756:3,476. Yikes! *That* doesn't look like much help. Let's make that more simple.

Look at the two numbers again. You can see that the Earth is bigger than the moon. (12,756 is bigger than 3,476.) How many times bigger? Let's find out. Here's where your calculator might come in handy. Divide the size of the Earth by the size of the moon.

$$3{,}476 \overline{)12{,}756} \quad 3.67$$

You've just figured out that the Earth is 3.67 times bigger than the moon. In other words, the ratio of the size of Earth to the size of the moon is 3.67:1 ("3.67 to 1"). The ratio 3.67:1 is the same as 12,756:3,476. It's sure a lot more simple though, isn't it?

Now you know two important things about your model. First, you know that you want the Earth to be the size of a basketball. Second, you know that the Earth is 3.67 times bigger than the moon. Or you can twist it around. You can say the moon is 3.67 times *smaller* than the Earth.

STEP THREE. You have a model for the Earth — a basketball. Ask yourself, "What is 3.67 times smaller than a basketball?"

How can you find that out? First you need to know how big a basketball is. Find one and measure it. You could hold a ruler up to the basketball and try to guess its diameter. But that can be tricky. There's a better way. You can measure the distance *around* the ball. Then you can use that number to figure out the ball's width. Wrap a tape measure around the middle of the ball. Or use a piece of string and then measure the length of the string.

Now you need to learn a new number. The number is 3.14. People use this number all the time to find out the diameter, or the width, of circles, and spheres. How do they do that? First they measure the circumference, which is the distance around a sphere. Then they divide the circumference by 3.14. That tells them the diameter. No matter what the circumference is — it can be big or small — dividing it by 3.14 will give you the diameter.

You've just discovered one of nature's most important ratios. The ratio of any circle's (or sphere's) circumference to its diameter is 3.14:1. No matter how big or small the circle or sphere is, it's circumference is *always* 3.14 times bigger.

Now let's go back to our model. The circumference of a basketball is 76.2 cm. ("Cm" stands for centimeters.) Divide 76.2 by 3.14.

$$3.14 \overline{)76.2} \quad 24.3$$

Did you get 24.3? That's the diameter of a basketball. A basketball is 24.3 cm wide.

So then, how big will your model moon be? Earlier, you found out that the moon is 3.67 times smaller than the Earth. Your model Earth is a basketball about 24.3 cm wide. What is 3.67 times smaller than that? Let's find out.

$$3.67 \overline{)24.3} \quad 6.6$$

You want your model of the moon to be 6.6 cm wide. Can you think of a ball that's about 6.6 cm wide? Here is a list of some different balls and their diameters:

Basketball	**24.3cm**
Soccer ball	**21.8 cm**
Softball	**9.7 cm**
Baseball	**7.3 cm**
Tennis ball	**6.5 cm**
Golf ball	**4.4 cm**
Marble	**1.0 cm**

Which one is closest to being 6.6 cm wide? A tennis ball. A tennis ball is 6.5 cm wide. You can use a tennis ball as your model moon.

Congratulations! You've just finished the first part of your model. If the Earth were shrunk to the size of a basketball, then the moon would be about the size of a tennis ball. Your new models of the Earth and moon are small enough to hold in your hands. Now you can get a feel for their different sizes.

Now we want to know where to put your model Earth and moon. But before we do, let's make a guess. How close do you think your

model moon should be to the Earth? Are they right next to each other? Or are they across the room from each other? Make your best guess. Then we'll finish the model and see how close you came.

STEP FOUR. To begin step four, ask yourself a question. "At the scale I've been using, what is the distance from the Earth to the moon?" That's easy enough. The scale for your model is that the Earth is the size of a basketball. How many basketball-widths is the moon from the Earth?

In real distances, the moon is 384,500 km from the Earth. The Earth is 12,756 km wide. Time for another ratio. The ratio of the moon's *distance* to the Earth's *diameter* is 384,500:12,756. Let's make that easier to understand.

Divide 384,500 by 12,756.

$$12{,}756 \overline{\smash{)}384{,}500} \quad 30.14$$

Go ahead and round 30.14 down to 30. This is much better. Now you can say that the ratio of the moon's distance to the Earth's diameter is 30:1. The moon is 30 times farther away from the Earth than the Earth is wide. How wide is your basketball? You figured that out earlier. It's 24.3 cm. What is 30 times that number?

$$\begin{array}{r} 24.3 \text{ cm} \\ \times\ 30 \\ \hline 729 \text{ cm} \end{array}$$

Seven hundred and twenty-nine centimeters is the same as 7.29 meters. Round that up to 7.3 meters. Your tennis ball moon should be 7.3 meters from your basketball Earth. That's about 24 feet.

Now you've got all the measurements you need for your model. But let's not build it yet. Let's look at another way to describe the scale you're using.

You know that a 24.3 cm basketball is a model of a 12,756 km Earth. Divide 12,756 by 24.3.

$$24.3 \overline{)12{,}756} = 524.9$$

Go ahead and round up to 525. You've just figured out that one centimeter of your model equals about 525 km in the real world.

1 cm = 525 km

This is a new way of describing the scale of your model. Remember that a kilometer equals 1,000 meters. A meter equals 100 centimeters. Now look at the next five sentences:

"In my model the Earth (12,756 km) is shrunk to the size of a basketball (24.3 cm)."

"One centimeter of my model equals 525 kilometers."

"One centimeter of my model equals 525,000 meters."

"One centimeter of my model equals 52,500,000 centimeters."

"The scale of my model is 1:52,500,000."

Each of those five sentences says exactly the same thing. You've found the true scale of your model. It's 1:52.5 million, or "one to 52.5 million."

Use this new scale to check your distance between the Earth and the moon. The real distance is 384,500 km. Your model should be 52.5 million times smaller than that.

$$52,500,000 \overline{) \, 384,500 \text{ km}} = 0.00732 \text{ km}$$

There are 1,000 meters in a kilometer. Now multiply 0.00732 by 1,000.

$$\begin{array}{r} 0.00732 \text{ km} \\ \times \, 1,000 \\ \hline 7.32 \text{ meters} \end{array}$$

Did you get it right? Earlier, you figured the distance between the Earth and the moon with Earth-diameters. You got a distance of 7.29 meters. Then you figured it with your new scale. You got a distance of 7.32 meters. That's a difference of only 0.03 meters. That's just 3 millimeters. I'd say you're right on the money.

STEP FIVE. Now for the fun part. Get a basketball, a tennis ball, and a long tape measure. Set up your Earth and moon at the right distance, about 7.3 meters. Is the moon closer to the Earth than you thought it would be? Farther away?

At the scale you are using, a tiny model space shuttle would orbit your model Earth (basketball) about 5 millimeters above its surface.

Now think about this: From 1968 to 1972, *nine* Apollo spacecraft carried 27 astronauts from Earth to the moon and back. Now that you've made your model, you can see how amazing those flights to the moon were.

Congratulations! You've finished your model! You've made a scale model of the Earth and the moon. You've placed them at the correct scale distance from each other.

A MODEL OF MARS

What's next? On to Mars! Use the same scale. How big would Mars be? How far away would it be? Mars has a diameter of 6,787 km. So it's smaller than Earth. Divide the size of Mars into the size of Earth.

$$\begin{array}{r} 1.9 \\ \hline 6{,}787\text{ km (Mars)} \,\big|\, 12{,}756\text{ km (Earth)} \end{array}$$

Round it off to an even 2. The ratio of the diameter of Mars to the diameter of Earth is 1:2. Earth is about twice the size of Mars. You can also say that Mars is about half the diameter of Earth. Now think about your model. How wide is your basketball? About 24 cm. So half the diameter of your basketball is about 12 cm. Look at the list of balls on page 16. The closest one is a softball, 9.7 cm. That's close, but not quite big enough. What else can you use? How about a cantaloupe or a large grapefruit? That would be just about right.

Now then, what about the distance to Mars? Remember, planets orbit around the sun. Their distances from each other change as they move. At its closest, Mars is about 59 million kilometers from Earth. Remember the ratio for your model? Your model is 52.5 million times smaller than the real Earth and moon. Use this same scale. How far away is Mars when it is closest to Earth? On your scale, it would be 52.5 million times smaller than 59 million kilometers. How do you figure that out? Divide 59,000,000 km by 52,500,000

$$52{,}500{,}000 \overline{)\,59{,}000{,}000 \text{ km}} \;\;\; 1.12 \text{ km}$$

Your answer is 1.12 km. That means that in your model of Mars (your cantaloupe or grapefruit) would be more than one kilometer away from your basketball! A kilometer is about six-tenths of a mile. And that's when Earth and Mars are closest together! When they're far apart, Mars would be more than seven kilometers away. That's four and a half miles!

Your model helps you see why a trip to Mars would take many months. A trip to the moon takes only a few days.

Now let's create the rest of the planets in the solar system. But wait. Could you do it at this scale? Yes and no. Yes, you can figure out the sizes and distances. But no, you can't actually build the models. Here's why. Using your scale, here are some of the sizes you'd need:

A sun that was 26.5 meters (87 feet) tall and 2.9 km (1.8 miles) away.

A Jupiter that was 2.7 meters (9 feet) tall and at least 12 km (7.5 miles) away.

A Pluto that was 4 cm (1 3/4 inches) wide but 86 km (53 miles) from your Earth.

It looks like the scale you used for the Earth and moon isn't going to work for the rest of the solar system. The solar system is just too big.

MAKING A NEW SCALE

But you don't have to give up yet. Just shrink the scale down. Make everything smaller. Then you can get it all to fit inside a small area.

Let's start with Pluto. That will help you make a good model of the solar system. Pluto is usually the farthest planet from the sun. Pluto's orbit around the sun is kind of odd. Sometimes it moves closer to the sun than Neptune does. To keep the model simple, let's use Pluto's average distance from the sun.

Before we do that, though, we need a new way to measure distances in the solar system. You measured the distance to the moon as 384,500 km. That's OK. Most calculators can handle that. But now you have to measure distances that are much larger. Pluto's average distance from the sun is 5,900,000,000 km. That's "5 billion 900 million" km. A lot of calculators can't handle numbers that big.

There's a better way. Don't figure how many kilometers a planet is from the sun. Instead figure how many times farther away it is from the sun than the Earth is. Here's an example. We know that the Earth is 150 million km from the sun. We call that one **Astronomical Unit**, or one "A.U." for short. One Astronomical Unit equals 150,000,000 km. You've created another ratio. The ratio between A.U.s and kilometers is 1:150,000,000.

Now look again at Pluto's distance from the sun. It's 5,900,000,000 km. One A.U. is 150,000,000 km. You can find out how many A.U.s Pluto is from the sun. Just divide 5,900,000,000 by 150,000,000.

$$150,000,000 \overline{)5,900,000,000} = 39.3$$

We'll round that to 40. Now you don't have such a huge number for Pluto's distance from the sun. Instead you can say that Pluto is about 40 A.U.s from the sun. This is the same as saying Pluto is 40 times farther from the sun than the Earth is.

Astronomers use A.U.s to measure all sorts of distances around the solar system. Here's a list of the planets in our solar system. It shows how far they are from the sun:

Planet	Distance (A.U.)
Mercury	0.4
Venus	0.7
Earth	1.0
Mars	1.5
Jupiter	5.2
Saturn	9.5
Uranus	19.2
Neptune	30.1
Pluto	39.5

This will help you to make a new scale for your model of the solar system. Shrink the solar system down. Make one A.U. equal to one meter. Now just substitute "meter" for

"A.U." Your new model of the solar system practically puts itself together for you. Earth is one A.U. from the sun in the "real" solar system. In your model it is now only one meter from the Sun. Mercury is four-tenths of a meter from the Sun. That's 40 centimeters. Jupiter is 5.2 meters from the sun. Saturn is 9.5 meters from the sun. And so on. Your whole model will fit inside 40 meters. You can fit that in your school playground or a park. Use a long string or a tape measure. Lay out your model. Maybe you've got a nice long piece of sidewalk nearby. You can lay out your model solar system on the sidewalk with chalk. Use the distances in our list of planets. All you have to do is measure in meters instead of A.U.s.

COMPARING SCALES

Now you have the distances between the planets small enough to work with. But how big should you make the planets? Get ready for a surprise. The planets of our solar system are very far apart. The planets practically shrink out of sight at the scale we've just used. In your first scale, the planets were large enough to look at. But the distances between them were too big to work with. Now you've got the distances shorter, but the planets are small. How small? You can figure that out for yourself.

For this model you've created a scale. One meter equals 150,000,000 kilometers. A kilometer is a thousand times longer than a meter. That means in your scale 1 meter equals 150,000,000,000 meters. The number 150,000,000,000 is 150 billion. Your scale is 1:150 billion. Everything in your model is shrunk so that it is 150 billion times smaller than normal.

How big is the sun at this scale? In the real solar system the sun is 1.4 million kilometers wide. In your model solar system it is 150 billion times smaller. How big would that be? A model sun in your solar system would be about one centimeter wide. That's the size of a small marble. Remember that the sun is the largest object in the solar system. It looks like your model planets are going to be *very* small indeed. How small? Look at a ruler marked in millimeters. Jupiter, the largest planet, would be a dot only one millimeter wide. It would look like this: •. Earth would be less than a tenth of a millimeter wide. You could put eleven Earths side by side in the tiny dot that is Jupiter.

Does this mean your model solar system isn't working? No. It's working fine. Just don't worry about the *sizes* of the planets. This model helps you picture how the planets are arranged around the sun.

Mercury, Venus, Earth, and Mars are called the "inner planets." Look at your model. You can see that they all huddle very close to the sun. Jupiter, Saturn, Uranus, Neptune, and Pluto are called the "outer planets." Look at Jupiter. It's 5.2 meters from the sun. Your solar system is 40 meters wide. Jupiter is called an "outer" planet. But it's only one-eighth of the way out from the center of the solar system. Saturn is 9.5 meters from the sun. It's only one-fourth of the way out from the center of the solar system. Finally you reach Uranus. Uranus is 19.2 meters from the sun. And it's still only half-way to Pluto, the farthest planet.

Look at the model again. Jupiter is at 5.2 meters from the sun. Saturn is at 9.5 meters from the sun. It is just about as far from the Sun to Jupiter as it is from Jupiter to Saturn! Now look at Saturn and Uranus. It is farther from Saturn to Uranus than it is from the sun to Saturn!

Now think about the Voyager II spacecraft. It left Earth in 1977. It reached Jupiter in 1979. It reached Saturn in 1981, Uranus in 1986, and Neptune in 1989. Now you can appreciate another part of your model. The Voyager II spacecraft traveled at more than 60,000 kilometers per hour. It took 12 years to travel the 30 meters between your tiny model Earth out to a tiny model Neptune.

Light travels very fast. It can circle the Earth seven times in one second. That's 300,000 km (186,000 miles) each *second*. When Voyager II passed Neptune, it sent radio signals to reach Earth. The signals traveled at the speed of light. They took more than four *hours* to get here.

Your scale model of the solar system is very small. You would have to take four hours walking from Earth to Neptune to show the correct scale for the speed of light. On your scale, the speed of light is 12 cm per minute. On your scale, a snail would travel at the speed of light. Now you've done something really amazing. You've made a snail's pace the fastest speed in the universe!

TRAVELING TO THE STARS

What about traveling to the stars? Scrunch your solar system down again. Before, you made one meter equal one A.U. This time, make one centimeter equal one A.U. That shrinks your solar system down so small that the sun is only a tenth of a millimeter wide. Pluto is only about 40 cm away from it. How small is your solar system now? It's so small that it can fit on a table top. Your scale before was 1:150 billion. Now it's 1:15 *trillion*. That's a hundred times smaller.

The closest star to our solar system is Alpha Centauri. It's 4.3 light-years away. One **light-year** is about 9.5 trillion kilometers. How many kilometers is 4.3 light-years? You can figure it out.

$$\begin{array}{r} \textbf{9.5 trillion km} \\ \textbf{x 4.3} \\ \hline \textbf{40.9 trillion km} \end{array}$$

Round that to 41 trillion km. This is your new super-small scale. At a scale of 1:15 trillion, Alpha Centauri is 15 trillion times closer. Forty-one trillion km divided by 15 trillion is the same as 41 divided by 15.

$$15\overline{)41} \quad 2.7$$

At this super-small scale, Alpha Centauri is 2.7 km away. That's 1.7 miles.

Think of it. In this scale, our solar system would fit on top of a table. But the nearest star is close to three kilometers away. What's in between our solar system and Alpha Centauri? Nothing really. There might be a handful of icy comets drifting around out past Pluto. After that, not much else. Space is called "space" for a very good reason. It's mostly empty.

Light from our sun takes 4.3 years to reach Alpha Centauri. If Voyager II was heading in that direction it would take about 20,000 *years* to get there.

Imagine taking 20,000 years to go 2.7 km to Alpha Centauri in your model. You'd be traveling as fast as a "scale" rocket ship. Imagine taking four years and four months to get there. That is the "scale" speed of light. A slow walk across 2.7 km would take about an hour. On your scale, your slow walking speed would be 40,000 times faster than the speed of light.

A SCALE IN DIFFERENT UNITS

There is another scale for comparing distances to the stars. It gives you a better feeling for just how close the planets are around the sun.

First we'll give you some numbers. One light-year equals 9.47 trillion km. That is how far light will travel in one year. One A.U. equals 150 million km. Remember, one A.U. is the distance from the sun to the Earth. Now, how would you find the number of A.U.s in a light-year? Divide 9.47 trillion by 150 million:

$$150{,}000{,}000 \overline{) 9{,}470{,}000{,}000{,}000 } \quad 63{,}115$$

There are 63,115 A.U.s in a light-year.

We've been using the metric system of measurement so far. That's kilometers and meters and centimeters. Now it's time for a change to English units. That's miles and feet and inches. Something very interesting happens when you compare inches to miles and A.U.s to light-years.

Here are a few more measurements. One mile is 5,280 feet long. One foot is 12 inches. How would you find the number of inches in a mile? You multiply 5,280 by 12.

5,280
x 12
63,360

There are 63,360 inches in a mile.

Look at that! There are 63,360 inches in a mile. There are 63,115 A.U.s in a light-year. The two numbers are very close to being the same. The difference isn't big enough to worry about. There are about as many inches in a mile as there are A.U.s in a light year.

Now you can compare distances between planets and stars. This is your scale: "When light-years are shrunk to miles, A.U.s are shrunk to inches."

Suppose you're looking at Saturn in the sky. Saturn is about 10 A.U.s away from you. Then you look at the North Star. The North Star is about 460 light-years away. Now use your new scale. Shrink the distance to Saturn so that 10 A.U.s is 10 inches. Then shrink the distance to the North Star so that 460 light-years is 460 miles. If you put Saturn 10 inches in front of your nose, the North Star would be as far away as San Diego, California, is from San Francisco, California. You can try other distances, too. At this scale, Neptune is an arm's length away (30 inches). Alpha Centauri is 4.3 miles from you. When you know the distance to the planets in A.U.s and the distances to a few stars in light-years, you can get a feeling for the huge emptiness between the stars.

LOOKING AT THE GALAXY

Let's push on. What about the whole **Milky Way** galaxy? After all, our sun is only one of hundreds of billions of stars swirling around in our galaxy. What would the Milky Way be like at the scale we've been using?

Here are a few more numbers. Our galaxy is about 100,000 light-years across. Our solar system is about 30,000 light-years from the center of the galaxy. It's about 20,000 light-years from the outside edge of the galaxy.

Go back to your scale of 1:15 trillion. That's the one you used to find out how far away Alpha Centauri is. At that scale, the whole solar system can fit on a table top. The Sun is a tenth of a millimeter wide. That's about the size of a speck of dust. Even at that scale, our galaxy is still five times bigger than the whole world! A scale of 1:15 trillion is *still* too big. We can't picture the size of the galaxy.

Shrink the universe again. Make it 10 times smaller. Now your scale is 1:150 trillion. The whole solar system is now about 8 cm wide. That's just 3 inches. This new solar system would fit inside an orange. At this scale, Alpha Centauri is 270 meters away.

Now use your new scale for the Milky Way. At this scale, our galaxy shrinks to the size of North America. One edge of it reaches to northern Alaska. The other edge covers southern Mexico. Scattered across this model of our galaxy are a few hundred billion stars. Each star is smaller than a speck of dust. The average distance between each star is longer than two football fields. In between all of these stars is a huge emptiness.

Here is your model of the Milky Way, our home galaxy. It covers a continent. But it is mostly empty space. One of those tiny points of light is our sun. Our super-tiny model Earth is only one millimeter from the sun. The sun's light takes over eight minutes to travel that one millimeter to the model Earth.

We're not quite finished. Scrunch the universe one last time. Shrink your scale 10 million times smaller. Your scale is now 1:1,500,000,000,000,000,000,000. That's a scale of one to 1.5 *billion-trillion*. In the real universe, the Milky Way is about 100,000 light-years wide. In this model, the Milky Way is now only 63 cm wide. That's 25 inches. Our galaxy is 1.5 billion-trillion times smaller. It is small enough to sit on a table top.

The Milky Way is only one galaxy. We think about 100 billion other galaxies exist in the universe. How far away are the other galaxies?

The Andromeda galaxy is 2.2 million light-years away from us. Use your new scale. A distance of 2.2 million light-years is shrunk to 14 meters. Light takes more than two million years to travel the 14 meters between these two model galaxies. The Andromeda galaxy is the *closest* large galaxy to our own.

Other galaxies are much farther away. There is a large cluster of about 1,000 galaxies called the Virgo cluster. It is 50 million light-years away. At this scale, it would be 320 meters from your table-top Milky Way. That's 1,050 feet. Distant galaxies are still farther. They are dozens of kilometers away.

Between the galaxies is an emptiness like nothing else in the universe. Galaxies are separated by enormous distances. Light takes many millions, even billions of years to go between them.

Some night look up at a star-filled sky. Now you understand just how huge outer space is. The Earth is large only to us living on it. Compared to the rest of space, it is incredibly small. See all those twinkling points of light above you? They are separated by enormous distances.

Some of the lights you see are planets. You know that the space between them is huge. Some of the lights are stars. You know that the stars are even farther from us than the planets. You know that the stars in our galaxy are far, far apart. Beyond our galaxy there are other galaxies. They are separated from us by even more enormous distances.

You have a feeling for how big space is. Not because you read numbers in a book. You know how big space is because you've made a model of it.

GLOSSARY

Astronomical Unit (A.U.): The average distance from the Earth to the sun. One A.U. equals 150,000,000 (150 million) kilometers, or 93,000,000 (93 million) miles.

Circumference: The distance around a circle or sphere.

Diameter: The width of a circle or a sphere, measured through its center.

Light-year: The distance that a beam of light can travel in one year. A light year is equal to 9,500,000,000,000 (9.5 trillion) kilometers, or 5,880,000,000,000 (5.88 trillion) miles.

Milky Way: The galaxy, or large group of stars, that contains our solar system.

Ratio: A set of numbers that compares one number to another.

Scale: The size of a model compared to the actual size of the thing being modeled.

Sphere: A perfectly round ball.